P9-BHY-214

CALGARY PUBLIC LIBRARY

FEB — — 2010

When Grandfather climbed the porch stairs carrying his old fiddle, I knew he had come for a special reason. He sat at the kitchen table and laid the fiddle carefully down in front of him.

"I'm going to give you this fiddle, my girl, but it comes with a story."

I pulled my chair closer to Grandfather. He gently picked up the fiddle and held it in his hands, turning it over and admiring it before placing it again on the table.

"Many years ago, before this was a country named Canada, a Metis family lived on a small river lot that ran deep into the bush. Other families lived on either side of them along that river.

Gabriel and Marie were your great, great, great grandparents, and they had two boys, Pierre and Louis, and two girls, Gabriella and Jeanette. Another baby was coming that spring.

Everything that Gabriel and Marie needed was found in the bush surrounding their small cabin. Every day they gathered berries, roots and medicinal plants from the forest, fish from the river, water to drink and wood to keep the stove burning. They also snared rabbits and hunted larger game.

Once a month or so, they travelled to neighbouring Metis communities down river or across the lakes to talk, laugh and dance with friends and relatives.

So, for many years, Gabriel went into the bush to bring food home to his family. He often followed the same path, and there, along the way, Gabriel had a very special friend.

Gabriel's friend was a tall spruce tree named Old Spruce. Everyday, as Gabriel made his way through the bush, he stopped to talk to the wise old tree. Gabriel shared news about his family and Old Spruce talked about the changes he saw happening over the years.

Sometimes Gabriel would bring his old fiddle and sit on the ground, leaning up against Old Spruce. He played many jigs and reels. He played his favourite tune, **Old Paint**. He also played a tune he wrote just for Old Spruce called **The Route**.

He practiced them because everyone liked to jig to the fiddle when the community gathered together. Old Spruce liked to hear **Lady Do Si Doe**, but Gabriel always saved Old Spruce's favourite tune, **Quadrille Waltz**, for the very end, just before he left to go home.

Old Spruce was already very old when Gabriel first began sitting and talking to him. One day, Old Spruce whispered to Gabriel in his raspy, barky voice,

'Gabriel, my friend, do a favour for me.'

'I would do anything for you,' replied Gabriel earnestly. 'What do you want?'

'I am old,' whispered Old Spruce. 'I am not going to live through another long winter. This will be my last season.'

Gabriel jumped up to face Old Spruce. 'Don't talk nonsense. You are strong and healthy. Your branches reach out and your needles are green.'

'Gabriel,' said Old Spruce. 'You must listen to me. I am old. I can feel even the smallest changes inside my body. I have lost many friends around me: spruce trees, poplar trees, and birch trees. It is my time to go. I ask you to do something that will keep my spirit alive in your family.'

'This fall after the first frost,' said Old Spruce, 'my needles will turn red and they will blow away with the wind. My breath will leave me, but my spirit will remain in my wood. I want you to cut me down and make a special fiddle out of my wood to play the jigs and reels that make people dance and laugh and celebrate.'

Gabriel stood proudly in front of Old Spruce.

'I will do as you ask, my friend. I will make the most beautiful fiddle. I will play music all night until the sun comes up. People will dance to the **Old Reel of Eight, The Old Man and the Old Woman**, and the **St. Anne's Reel**. I will make people laugh and sing.'

'One more thing,' said Old Spruce. 'You will have much wood left over. Use it to make furniture for your family, and with the shavings and scraps, make fires in the winter to keep your family warm.'

'Old Spruce,' said Gabriel, 'I will remember you
and miss you every time I play your fiddle.'"

Grandfather again carefully picked up the fiddle
in front of him and held it gently.

"That fall after the first frost," continued Grandfather, "just as Old Spruce said, the needles on his branches turned red and blew away with the wind. Old Spruce looked cold and bare. Gabriel came with his family to make a tobacco offering to the grandfathers from the four directions and to the spirit of life force in the old tree before cutting and hauling Old Spruce to the cabin.

At the cabin, Gabriel cut the wood into boards and planks. He made a beautiful crib for the new baby expected in the spring. He made a kitchen table with smoothly carved legs.

Then he began to work on the fiddle. He whistled jigs and reels as he carved and sanded late into the night.

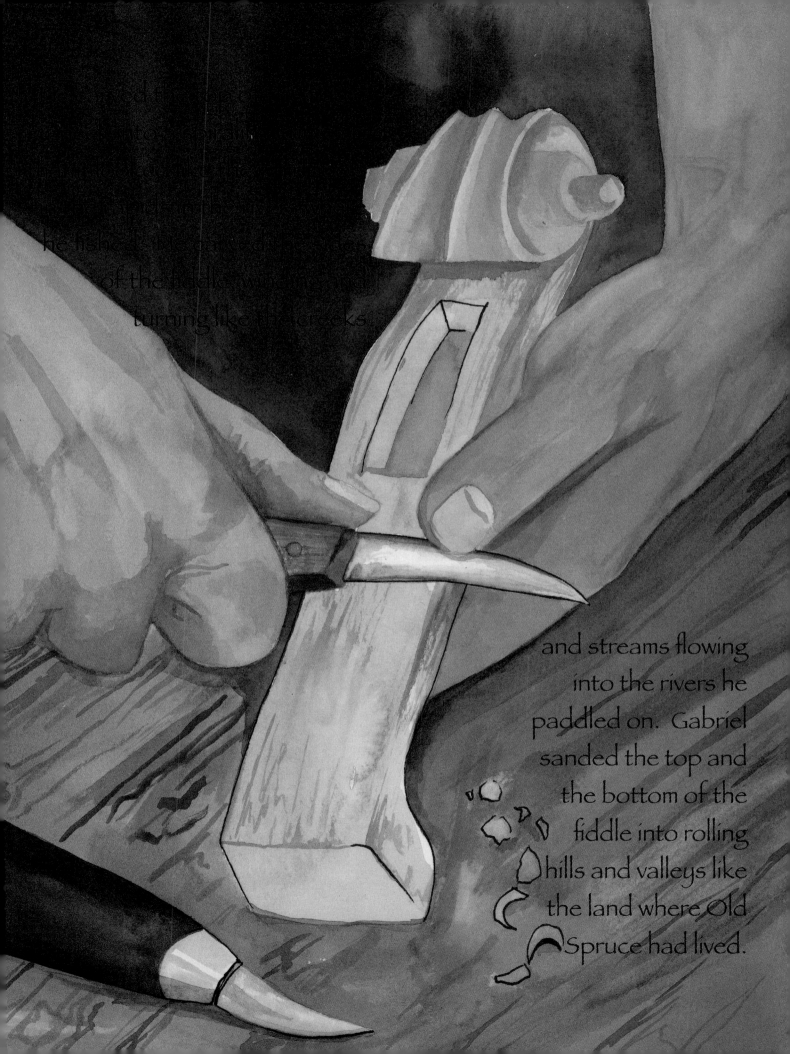

he fished the carved beauty
of the fiddle winding and
turning like the creeks

and streams flowing
into the rivers he
paddled on. Gabriel
sanded the top and
the bottom of the
fiddle into rolling
hills and valleys like
the land where Old
Spruce had lived.

Finally, Gabriel engraved a picture of Old Spruce standing strong and tall on the back of the fiddle.

Gabriel held the fiddle up into the light and plucked the strings, cocking his ear. Then he drew his bow across the strings to test the tone. It was magical. Old Spruce was alive in the sound of the strings.

Gabriel called the children and Marie to the kitchen table, and they gathered around to listen.

'My children, when I play the first song on Old Spruce, you will want to dance. Don't be shy! Let your feet fly across the floor! I am going to play a tune dedicated to your mother. My people came from the north, where we jig to a tune called **Big John McNeil**. Your mother's people come from the south, where they jig to a tune called the **Red River Jig**. In honour of your beautiful mother, my first song will be the Red River Jig.'

With that, Gabriel's arm shot out and the bow cracked across the strings like lightning in a summer storm. Gabriel made quick, confident strokes and tapped his feet: boom-chickee-boom-chickee-boom! White rosin powder rose off the bow into the air. What a beautiful sounding fiddle!

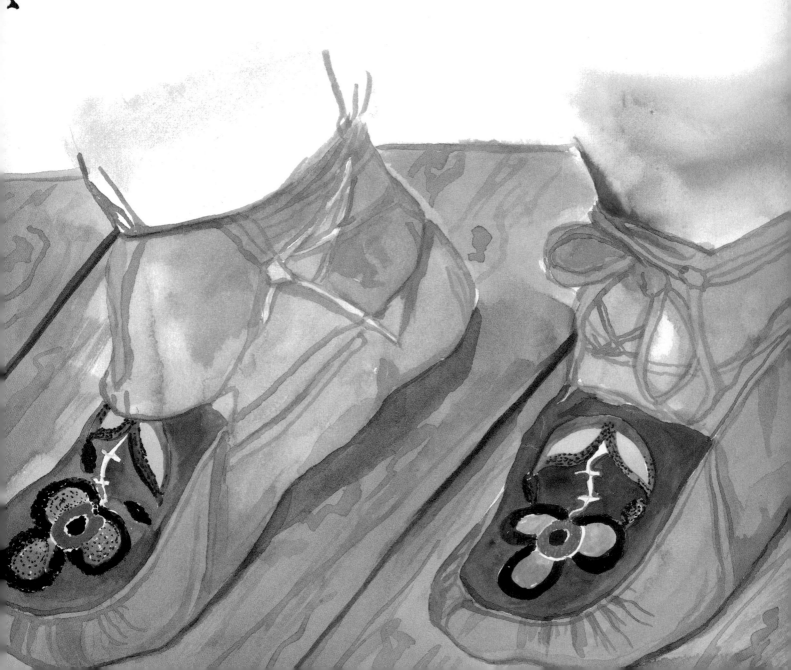

The children jumped up and started to jig, kicking their moccasins into the air. Marie clapped and laughed while the children danced. Gabriel almost knocked the water pail over! Out of breath, the children sat down around Gabriel to listen to Old Spruce's favourite tune, Quadrille Waltz.

For many years, Old Spruce sang for the people, who danced and laughed through the nights and into the mornings. Many shoes and moccasins were worn out on the wooden floors dancing to the sound of Old Spruce.

When Gabriel was very old, he passed the fiddle on to his children, who in turn passed it on to their children. Every time the fiddle passes from one generation to the next, the story I have just told you about Old Spruce is repeated.

This is why I am here, Andrea. I am telling you the story of Old Spruce because I am passing this fiddle on to you. You will continue to make Old Spruce sing so that the people can dance."

And that is the story that my grandfather told me the day he climbed the porch stairs carrying his old fiddle. My dad is teaching me how to play on Old Spruce. My very first song was **Twinkle Twinkle Little Star**.

My dad is now teaching me the **Gravel Road Jig**. I am going to learn to play **Rubber Dolly** and **Chase Me Charlie**. After I have mastered these songs I will learn **Devil's Dream** and of course Quadrille Waltz. Oh, there are so many tunes to learn!

My dad is teaching me how to play like the old Metis fiddlers, fast and with a jump that makes everyone want to dance. My dad says that Metis fiddle music is for one purpose: dancing.

When I learn to play Big John McNeil on Old Spruce, we will make everyone dance all night long.

The End

- Tabs -

twinkle twinkle little star

```
E        00110           00        00        00110
A   00        3322110   33221   33221 00     3322110
D
G
```

Gravel Road Jig

```
E  0123           00 0123                  00
A     2022 1321        2022 132100 00012222 1321   00012222 132100
D
G
```

Rubber Dolly

```
E                    00                      00
A   210      012    012    32122  210    012    012   32100
D      22       11                   22       11
G
```

Chase me charlie

```
E  0        01 0           0         01  0
A    23221023    23221011   23221023      23212100
D
G
```

```
E  030103010         030103010
A            23221011          23212100
D
G
```

- Song List -

Old Paint
The Route
Lady Do Si Doe
Quadrille Waltz
Old Reel of Eight
The Old Man and The Old Woman
St. Anne's Reel
Big John McNeil
Red River Jig

- Teaching Songs -

Twinkle Twinkle Little Star (slow)
Twinkle Twinkle Little Star (fast)
Gravel Road Jig (slow)
Gravel Road Jig (fast)
Rubber Dolly (slow)
Rubber Dolly (fast)
Chase Me Charlie (slow)
Chase Me Charlie (medium)
Chase Me Charlie (fast)
Devil's Dream (slow)
Devil's Dream (medium)
Devil's Dream (fast)
Big John McNeil (slow)
Big John McNeil (medium)
Big John McNeil (fast)

Andrea's Fiddle - Narrated by Susan Dupuis

Desmond Lagace is a multi-talented instrumentalist from Swan River, Manitoba who is very active in both music instruction and production. Music, carpentry, and mechanics are some of the wide variety of interests that keep him busy. A close connection to nature is good for his soul, but spending time with his wife Gina and children Chloe and Desi is paramount.